This book belongs to

....

The Puffin Book of Five-Minute Bear Stories

Kelly,

We hope you enjoyed your time at Meethill Nursery. Good luck in the future.

BBinc

The Puffin Book of Five-minute Bear Stories

Illustrated by Steve Cox

TED SMART

VIKING/PUFFIN

Published by the Penguin Group
Penguin Books Ltd, 27 Wrights Lane, London W8 5TZ, England
Penguin Putnam Inc., 375 Hudson Street, New York, New York 10014, USA
Penguin Books Australia Ltd, Ringwood, Victoria, Australia
Penguin Books Canada Ltd, 10 Alcorn Avenue, Toronto, Ontario, Canada M4V 3B2
Penguin Books (NZ) Ltd, Private Bag 102902, NSMC, Auckland, New Zealand

On the World Wide Web at: www.penguin.com

Penguin Books Ltd, Registered Offices: Harmondsworth, Middlesex, England

First published 2000
3 5 7 9 10 8 6 4 2

The moral right of the author and illustrator has been asserted

Set in 17 on 25pt Garamond 3

Made and printed in Italy by de Agostini

British Library Cataloguing in Publication Data
A CIP catalogue record for this book is available from the British Library

ISBN 0–670–89202–5

This edition produced for The Book People Ltd,
Hall Wood Avenue, Haydock, St Helens WA11 9UL

CONTENTS

BALDILOCKS AND THE SIX BEARS

Dick King-Smith

THERE WAS ONCE a magic forest and in it lived fairies, pixies, elves and goblins. Some of the goblins were full of mischief and some of the elves were rather spiteful, but on the whole, the fairy people were a happy lot. All except one.

He was a hobgoblin, not bad-looking; he might even have been thought handsome except for one thing. He hadn't a hair on his head.

Someone – probably an elf – had named him Baldilocks, and that was what everyone called him.

How sad he was. He envied all the other fairy people their fine locks, each time they met, at the full moon.

In a clearing among the trees was a huge fairy-ring, and in the middle sat the wisest fairy of them all, the Queen of the Forest.

As usual, everyone laughed when Balidlocks came into the fairy-ring.

'Baldilocks!' someone would shout, and then the pixies would titter and the elves would snigger and the goblins would chuckle and the fairies would giggle. All except one.

She was a little red-haired fairy, not specially beautiful but with such a kindly face. She alone did not laugh at the bald hobgoblin.

One night, the Queen of the Forest said to Baldilocks, 'Would you like to grow a fine head of hair?'

'Oh, I would, Your Majesty!' cried the hobgoblin. 'But how do I go about it?'

'Ask a bear,' said the Queen of the Forest, and not a word more would she say.

The very next morning Baldilocks set out to find a bear.

He soon came to a muddy pool where a big brown bear was catching frogs.

'Excuse me,' said Baldilocks. 'Could you tell me how to grow a fine head of hair?'

The brown bear looked carefully at the hobgoblin. He knew that the only way a bald person can grow hair is by rubbing bear's grease into his scalp. But he wasn't going to say that, because he knew that the only way to get bear's grease is to kill a bear and melt him down.

He picked up a pawful of mud.

'Rub this into your scalp,' said the brown bear.

So Baldilocks took the sticky mud and rubbed it on his head. But it didn't make one single hair grow.

The next bear Baldilocks met was a big black one. It was robbing a wild-bees' nest.

'Excuse me,' said Baldilocks. 'Could you tell me how to grow a fine head of hair?'

The black bear looked carefully at the hob-goblin. He pulled out a pawful of honeycomb.

'Rub this into your scalp,' said the black bear.

So Baldilocks took the honey and rubbed it into his head. It was horribly sticky, but it didn't make one single hair grow.

The third bear that Baldilocks met was a big gingery one that was digging for grubs in a nettle patch.

Baldilocks asked his question again, and the ginger bear pulled up a pawful of nettles and said, 'Rub these into your scalp.'

So Baldilocks took the nettles and rubbed them on his head. They stung him so much that his eyes began to water, but they didn't make one single hair grow.

The fourth bear that Baldilocks came across, a big chocolate-coloured one, was digging out an ants' nest and, by way of reply to the hobgoblin, he handed him a pawful of earth that was full of ants.

When Baldilocks rubbed it on his head, the ants bit him so hard that the tears rolled down his face, but they didn't make one single hair grow. Baldilocks found the fifth bear by the side of a river. It was a big old grey bear, and it was eating some rotten fish. When Baldilocks's question had been asked and answered, and he had rubbed the fish on his head, they made it smell perfectly awful. But, once again, they didn't

make one single hair grow.

Baldilocks had just about had enough.

He almost began to hope that he wouldn't meet another bear. But he did.

It was a baby bear, a little golden one, sitting in the sun.

'Excuse me,' said Baldilocks. 'Could you tell me how to grow a fine head of hair?'

The baby bear looked fearfully at the hobgoblin. He did not answer, so Baldilocks said, 'I expect you'll tell me to rub something into my scalp.'

'Yes,' said the baby bear in a small voice.

'What?'

'Bear's grease,' said the baby bear.

'Bear's grease?' said Baldilocks. 'How do I get hold of that?'

'You have to kill a bear,' said the baby bear in a whisper, 'and melt him down.'

'Oh no!' said Baldilocks.

When next the fairy people met, the Queen of the Forest said to Baldilocks, 'You haven't grown any hair. Didn't you ask a bear?'

'I asked six, Your Majesty,' said Baldilocks, 'before I found out that what I need is bear's grease, and to get that I would have to kill a bear and melt him down.'

'That might be difficult,' said the Queen of the Forest, 'but perhaps you could kill a little one?'

She smiled as she spoke, because she knew that high in a nearby tree a small golden bear sat listening anxiously.

'I couldn't do such a thing,' said Baldilocks. 'I'd sooner stay bald and unhappy.'

Up in the tree, the baby bear hugged himself silently.

After the others had gone away, Baldilocks still sat alone in the fairy-ring. At least he thought he was alone, till he looked round and saw the little red-haired fairy with the kindly face.

'I think,' she said, 'that bald people are much the nicest.'

'You do?' said Baldilocks.

'Yes. So you mustn't be unhappy any more. If you are, you will make me very sad.'

Baldilocks looked at her, and to his eyes, she was beautiful.

He smiled the happiest of smiles.

'You mustn't be sad,' he said. 'That's something I couldn't bear.'

URSULA BY THE SEA

Sheila Lavelle

URSULA HAD SIXTEEN teddy bears and she loved every one. But the one she loved most was Fredbear.

Fredbear had lost an eye and hadn't much fur left, but still Ursula loved him best of all.

She knitted him a red jumper to keep his bald tummy warm, and she sang him to sleep every night.

Ursula lived with her Aunt Prudence. One sunny morning she came downstairs and found her aunt in the kitchen, wearing a new yellow sun-dress.

Aunt Prudence was packing a picnic basket with ham

sandwiches, sausage rolls and chocolate cake.

'We're going to the seaside,' Aunt Prudence said.

'Hooray!' shouted Ursula. 'Have you packed me a currant bun?'

'Of course,' smiled Aunt Prudence. 'With your favourite filling of porridge oats and honey.'

Ursula ran to fetch her bucket and spade.

Aunt Prudence knew that Ursula loved bears. But she didn't know that Ursula had a very special secret.

Ursula's secret was a magic spell that could turn her from an ordinary girl into a *real, live bear*.

And all she needed was a currant bun, filled with porridge oats and honey.

Aunt Prudence put the picnic basket in the car. Fredbear sat on Ursula's knee and gazed out of the window. He looked very smart in his new red jumper.

The sun was shining and Ursula sang all the way to Sandy Bay.

Aunt Prudence parked the car and Ursula helped

to carry everything down to a quiet part of the beach.

'This looks like a nice place,' said Aunt Prudence.

Ursula looked at the waves sparkling in the sunshine.

'I'm going for a paddle,' she said.

'Be careful,' warned Aunt Prudence. 'I think the tide's coming in.'

Ursula ran over the warm sand towards the sea. She splashed in and out of the water and jumped over the waves.

After a while, Ursula began to build a sandcastle. It was the best sandcastle she had ever made.

When it was finished, Ursula sat Fredbear on the top. She made a flag from a lollipop stick and a paper hanky, and gave it to Fredbear to hold.

'Guard the castle, Fredbear,' she said. 'I'm going to buy an ice cream.'

The café was a long way across the beach and Ursula had to wait ages in the queue. On her way back, she heard children shouting and laughing. It was a Punch and Judy show and Ursula just had to stop and watch.

Ursula enjoyed herself so much that she forgot all about Fredbear. Then, all at once, she remembered.

She raced across the sand to where she had left him. Ursula stopped and stared.

There was no sandcastle, and no bucket and spade, and no Fredbear. The tide had come in and washed them all away.

Ursula gazed out to sea. She saw a few seagulls and a sailing boat with a white sail. Then she noticed a small red shape bobbing up and down in the water.

It was Fredbear.

Teddy bears can't swim and Ursula knew *she* couldn't swim that far. It would be stupid to try. And then all at once she had an idea.

'Teddy bears can't swim,' she said to herself. 'But *real* bears can!'

She dashed up the beach towards Aunt Prudence. Aunt Prudence was fast asleep in her deckchair, her knitting in her lap.

Ursula quickly opened the picnic basket and took out the currant bun with the special magic mixture. She hid among the rocks and began to gobble the bun as fast as she could.

'I'M A BEAR, I'M A BEAR, I'M A BEAR,' she mumbled. A seagull flying by almost dropped his fish in surprise. For Ursula had disappeared, and in her place a small brown bear was dancing about in the sand.

Ursula had turned into Ursula Bear.

Ursula Bear scampered back down the beach and splashed into the sea. She swam as hard as she could, to where Fredbear was now only a tiny red dot in the distance. The waves got up her nose and in her ears, but Ursula managed to reach Fredbear at last.

She was only just in time, for the water had soaked through his fur and he was beginning to sink. Ursula grabbed him and swam towards the shore. She ran along the beach with Fredbear safe in her arms. Now she had to turn back into a girl again, and this time she needed beefburger and chips to make the magic work.

There was only once place to get beefburger and chips, and that was the café.

Ursula peeped in at the back door of the café. There was nobody about, and she wondered if she dared go in. Suddenly she darted behind some dustbins as a boy came out with some scraps for the seagulls.

Beefburger and chips! Just what Ursula needed!

The boy went back inside and Ursula quickly snatched some of the food. She had to fight the seagulls over it, and they screamed in fury.

Then Ursula crouched behind the bins, to eat her few scraps. She grunted the magic words backwards as she chewed.

'RAEB A M'I, RAEB A M'I, RAEB A M'I,' she growled.

A minute later there was Ursula in her blue shorts and striped T-shirt, and quite herself again. She hurried back to her aunt.

Ursula took off Fredbear's wet jumper and sat him on a rock in the sunshine to dry. Aunt Prudence opened her eyes.

'What shall we do now, Ursula?' she said.

'Let's have lunch,' said Ursula. 'I'm starving!' And she began to spread the picnic out on the sand.

ELEPHANT'S LUNCH

Kate Walker

CLARA BEAR STARED into her schoolbag and frowned. 'Are you sure you've given me enough to eat?' she asked her mother.

'Enough?' her mother cried. 'You've got four peanut-butter sandwiches, six bananas, a piece of chocolate cake and an apple pie.'

'But I'll be at school *all* day,' said Clara, 'and I get awwwwfully hungry.'

'You won't get hungry,' her mother said. 'You couldn't possibly get hungry. You've got enough lunch in there to fill an elephant. Now off you go.'

'All right,' said Clara Bear. 'If you say so.' And she kissed her mother goodbye and set off for school.

Halfway there, Clara suddenly saw an elephant. He was standing on the other side of the railway line. Clara stopped and stared at him. The elephant stared back.

'Hello,' Clara said.

The elephant blinked and looked away along the tracks. Clara looked too. There was nothing coming.

'Are you waiting for a train?' she asked.

The elephant didn't answer.

'I waited for a train once,' said Clara, 'and it was late and I got awwwwwfully hungry. So hungry my tummy got angry and growled at me and made a pain. I hope your train isn't late because your tummy is much bigger than mine and you'll get an awfully big terrible pain.'

The elephant didn't say a word; his ears hung low.

Clara knew all about waiting for trains and how hungry that made you – more so than waiting for buses, or waiting for traffic lights to change. The elephant had to eat something. Clara opened her bag.

Elephants liked peanuts, everyone knew that, so she took out one of her peanut-butter sandwiches and offered it to him. But the elephant didn't take it; he just stared as blankly as before. 'Yummie, yummie, peanut butter!' Clara said and rubbed her tummy.

The elephant didn't seem to understand that she meant him to take it. So, to show him, she ate the first sandwich herself, making loud, enjoyable munching noises. Then she held out a second sandwich.

But again the elephant stared and didn't say a word.

Clara Bear ate the second sandwich, saying, 'Yummie yummie!' and rolling her eyes. But still the elephant didn't understand.

She ate the third one and licked her lips, 'Mmmmmm!'

The elephant raised his trunk and scratched his ear and simply looked away.

He wasn't a very smart elephant, Clara thought. 'If you don't eat this last yummie, delicious peanut-butter sandwich, I will.'

The elephant's trunk hung motionless.

'This is your last chance,' Clara said,

and raised the sandwich over her mouth.

'And this is your second last chance,' she lowered it down.

'And this is your third last chance.' She put it in her wide-open mouth.

The elephant looked away. Clara closed her mouth and the sandwich disappeared.

'You may not know this,' she said, 'but some trains are so late, they don't come at all. Imagine how hungry you'll get *then*!'

The elephant wiggled his ears slightly.

He's getting the message now, Clara thought. She delved into her bag and took out the six bananas, peeled them and laid them out on their skins for the elephant to take.

But the elephant looked away again. And now that the bananas were peeled, they had to be eaten. Clara sat down and munched her way through all six of them.

'You're the fussiest animal I've ever met,' she said. She peered into her school bag again. 'I suppose you like chocolate cake?' she asked.

Clara Bear looked along the railway track. There was still no train in sight. 'All right,' she said at last, 'I'll share my cake with you.'

She broke the chocolate cake in half and placed one piece on the railway track for the elephant to take. She went to put the other piece back into her bag, but couldn't resist taking just one small bite. Then another. And then just one more. And then there was only one bite left and that wasn't worth putting away. So Clara popped it into her mouth and the cake was gone.

In the distance she heard a train coming. It had to be the elephant's train! He wouldn't go hungry after all.

Clara snatched up the piece of cake and backed well away from the railway line to watch the train come through. It pulled up and stood for a minute, then blew its whistle and moved off again.

When it had passed, the elephant was gone. And so was the other piece of chocolate cake. Clara had gobbled it without thinking while watching the train pass through. Now all she had for an entire day's lunch was one not-very-big apple pie.

'Oh dear, I'm going to get awfully hungry at school,' she thought. Clara acted quickly. She gobbled the apple pie to make her bag as light as possible, then ran all the way home.

'Mummy, quick, I need some more lunch.' She held open her empty bag.

Her mother stared in disbelief. 'Clara, what happened to the lunch I gave you?'

'I ate it,' said Clara. 'I had to. You see, there was this elephant waiting for his train and . . .'

'So it was an elephant today,' her mother said.

'That's right,' said Clara, 'a big one.'

'Not a rhinoceros?' said her mother.

'No,' said Clara, 'that was yesterday that I met a rhinoceros.'

'And not a giraffe?'

'Don't you remember? That was the day before,' Clara smiled.

Mother Bear shook her head and started to make another lunch. 'I don't know where you put all this food, Clara,' she said.

'In my tummy, of course,' said Clara, 'so it won't growl at me and make a pain.'

'Well, I'm sorry to have to say this,' said her mother, a little annoyed, 'but, Clara, you eat like an elephant!'

'That's not true!' said Clara. 'I happen to know that elephants don't eat very much at all.'

And, oddly enough, neither do camels, as Clara found out on her way to school the next day.

NOT-SO-BLUE BEAR

Hiawyn Oram

ONCE, BLUEBIRD WAS a grey bird – as grey and dull as grey rock.

'This is no good for me,' she said. 'My nature is as clear and bright as the blue sky.'

One day she was flying over a lake.

The waters of the lake reflected the sky.

They were as blue as Greybird felt she should be. She dipped her head in the blue water and examined her reflection. Still as grey as grey.

Then she noticed a bright-blue butterfly fluttering near by.

'Oh, Butterfly,' she said. 'Tell me how you got to be so blue. I bet it was from dipping into this lake.'

'As a matter of fact,' fluttered the butterfly, 'it was. And if you follow my instructions exactly for just four mornings, then you too can be as blue as the blue lake.'

So Greybird listened to Butterfly's instructions and followed them exactly.

And on the fourth morning, when she fluttered out of the water, there she was – as blue as the bright, cloudless sky. She was about to fly away and show the world when she remembered Butterfly's last instruction.

'Blue lake, blue lake,' she sang,
'Thanks with all my heart,
Oh, thanks in every way
For giving me such beauty,
And turning me from grey.'

Then and only then, did she fly off
to admire herself in every pool and stream she came to.

A few days later, as she preened on the edge of the lake, along came Black Bear.

'Oh my, oh my, Bluebird!' he marvelled. 'As I remember it you were very recently a grey bird!'

'True,' warbled Bluebird. 'But what a transformation, huh?'

Black Bear sat down and took a good look at Bluebird. He looked down at his own fur.

And deep in his big shy heart, a thought occurred to him.

'If I were as blue as Bluebird, perhaps I'd stop being so shy. Perhaps I'd be able to preen and sing and show off. Perhaps if my appearance changed I'd change with it!'

And now that the thought had occurred to him, Black Bear couldn't get rid of it. It buzzed round him like a fly. Finally, very shyly, he spoke up.

'Er, Bluebird . . .' he mumbled. 'I don't suppose you'd share the secret of how you turned from dull grey to beautiful blue, er, would you?'

'Well, why not? Butterfly shared it with me,' trilled Bluebird. 'If you listen carefully and follow my instructions exactly, then you too can be as blue as blue.'

So Black Bear listened carefully and followed Butterfly's instructions.

He bathed in the blue water of the lake four times for four mornings. First facing north. Then facing south. Then facing east. Then facing west.

Each time he sang a song asking the lake for a little of its blue.

'Blue lake, blue lake,' he sang.
'Just enough to paint this fur
That makes me dark and shy,
Share with me your lovely blue
And Blue Bear will be I!'

And on the fourth morning, when he ambled out of the water, there he was – not Black Bear at all but Blue Bear – as bright and blue as the cloudless sky.

'Oh my, oh my!' he danced. 'This really is something, isn't it?'

He stared at his reflection in the lake. He blushed at his new blue beauty.

Then he rushed off to find buffalo and Wolf and Coyote and see if, for once in his life, he could

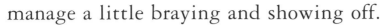

manage a little braying and showing off.

'Oh, black Buffalo, grey Wolf and grey Coyote!' he cried when he found them. 'Isn't it amazing? Have you ever seen anything like it?' He stood on his hind legs and did his best to prance.

'Even the ears! Even the claws! What do you think, my friends? What do you think?'

Buffalo and Wolf and Coyote stared at him as if he'd gone mad.

'Isn't WHAT amazing?' asked Buffalo.

'Even the ears, what?' asked Wolf.

'Even the claws, what?' asked Coyote.

Then Bear looked down at himself in dismay. There was the faintest tinge of blue at the tips of his claws. But the rest of

him was as black as black bark on a moonless night.

And at that moment Bluebird flew up and perched on one of Buffalo's horns.

'Oh, Bear!' she trilled breathlessly. 'I said follow my instructions exactly!'

'But I did,' said Bear sitting down in a heap of disappointment. 'Didn't I? Four times each morning, facing north, facing south . . .'

But even as the words came out of his mouth, he remembered. He'd done everything to get what he wanted from the lake but forgotten to sing his thanks on the fourth morning.

Then very slowly he got up and ambled off into the dark woods to think. And soon he had decided he was Black Bear after all, not Blue Bear. That's the way it was. That's the way it always would be.

'And considering I am shy and not a show-off,' he sighed, 'that's the way it always *should* be.'

THE DOG AND THE BEAR

Traditional

A LONG TIME AGO, in Russia, there was a dog who lived on a farm. He was very large and fierce and he growled so loudly that bad men who tried to steal a fat hen or a piglet dared not come any nearer. He was such a good guard dog that his master fed him well and often gave him a juicy bone to chew.

In time, the dog grew old. His teeth were not as sharp as they used to be and his growl was not as frightening. Sometimes he fell asleep and he didn't hear thieves creeping into the farm. One day, a fox slipped past the dog and killed several hens. His master was very angry.

'What use are you?' he scolded. 'I shall buy a young dog to replace you. Be off with you and find your own food – you'll get no more from me.'

The poor dog was very sad to be thrown out of his home. He had no idea where to go so he wandered off into the forest with his tail between his legs. He followed the trail of some mice and a hare but he caught nothing and as the days went by, he grew very hungry and weak.

As he was hiding in some bushes, feeling sorry for himself, a big brown bear came along. He caught sight of the dog and asked him what was the matter.

'My master has turned me out because I am old,' said the dog. 'I have been trying to find some food but I am so used to being fed that I have never learned to hunt for myself.'

'There is plenty to eat in the forest if you know where to

look,' said the bear. 'What about some honey or a handful of berries?'

'I don't think I would like honey, it's too sticky, and seeds and berries are for birds, not dogs.'

'Bears like them too and honey is delicious,' said the bear, licking his lips at the thought. 'However, everyone to his taste. Let's try hunting together. I am getting old too and I can no longer smell as well as I used to.'

So the two animals hunted together and shared everything they caught. Sometimes the bear caught fish for them both, but when he dug up anthills, the dog kept well away for the ants bit him and tickled his nose.

Hunting was hard work, so one day the dog said, 'Why don't we go to my master's house? He has a baby who lies in a cradle outside the kitchen door on sunny days. If you seize the child and run off with it, I'll chase after you and pretend to be very fierce. Then you must put the baby down and I will guard it until my master comes. He will be so pleased that I have saved the baby's life that he might feed me again. If he does, I shall be sure to save something for you.'

The bear agreed to the plan. On the next sunny day, the friends hid and watched the farm. Before long, the baby was brought outside and left in his cradle in the sunshine.

The huge bear made his way across the farmyard and picked up the child by his clothes. The old dog came chasing after him, making as much noise as possible. The bear dropped the baby and ran off but the dog stayed by the baby's side. When the farmer arrived, the child was howling with fright but he was unharmed. The new dog never came out at all as he was too frightened of the bear.

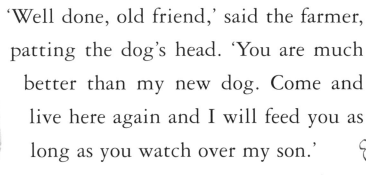

'Well done, old friend,' said the farmer, patting the dog's head. 'You are much better than my new dog. Come and live here again and I will feed you as long as you watch over my son.'

The dog trotted off to the farmhouse with his old master. He was fed every day and all he had to do was sit by the baby and bark fiercely now and then to show that he was awake. Each evening, the bear came to the back of the farmhouse and the dog gave him some food.

Time passed and one day the farmer's eldest daughter was to be married.

'Let me into the house,' said the bear to the dog. 'I love music and sweet cakes.'

'How can I let you in?' protested the dog. 'Someone will see you and I shall get into trouble and be turned out again.'

'No one will see me amongst so many guests,' said the bear 'I'll hide in a dark corner.' So the dog agreed to let his friend in.

All went well at first. The bear slipped into the house and sat in a corner and no one noticed him. But as the party got going, the fiddler began to play and everyone started dancing. The bear liked the music so much that he came out to join the other guests.

'Look, look, it's a bear!' shouted a frightened child. The guests began to scream and run about wildly and the bear was confused by the noise. He ran out of the house and the guests chased after him.

The bear didn't dare come near the farm again and the old dog missed him. He was bored too with minding the baby who pulled his tail and tweaked his ears. So one day, he wandered off into the forest to join his friend again. In time, the dog and the bear grew to be quite clever hunters and they never went hungry again.

BROWN BEAR IN A BROWN CHAIR

Irina Hale

THERE ONCE WAS a Brown Bear who lived in a brown chair. He was sat upon very often, because you couldn't see he was there.

'I'm feeling so flat,' he said, 'when really a bear should feel happy and fat.'

One day, he had a good idea, so he called Maggie, the little girl whose bear he was.

'I must have a ribbon round my neck,' he said, 'so that people can see I'm here.'

Maggie got him a yellow ribbon off a chocolate box. Bear

sat happily on his chair. A mother bird on the window-sill saw him. She cheeped to her children, 'Look! There's a bear in that room with no clothes on! Only a yellow ribbon round his neck, and nothing else!'

Bear began to feel he was wearing too little.

'I hope those nasty birds don't find any worms for breakfast today,' he said.

'I have to have some trousers now,' Bear told Maggie.

So she cut the legs off an old pair of stripy pants to Bear's size and hemmed them. But they were too tight and made his tummy stick out.

'Aren't I a well-dressed bear?' Bear said.

Just then, the cat went by and said, 'How can you be well-dressed if you don't have shoes on? Bears like you don't deserve to sit on comfy armchairs!'

(The cat really wanted the chair all to himself.)

Bear stamped his feet till Maggie came. 'I've got to have a pair of shoes now, or I'll never be really well-dressed.'

So Maggie had to take the shoes off her doll for Bear. The doll was very cross and gave a big sneeze. 'I shall get a bad cold now, all because of you!' she said to Bear. But he pretended not to hear.

Suddenly Bear saw a little mouse, peeping at him over the chair.

It squeaked, 'Oh what a fat, lazy bear! Just lying around on a chair all day! Not like us poor mice. We have to work hard just to find one tiny crumb!'

So Bear said to Maggie, 'Now I must have a shirt, to cover my tummy that's sticking out!'

Maggie sat down and made him a shirt, sewing with large stitches. It took a bit of time, but at last there it was, finished. Bear felt very proud.

'Am I dressed right, now?' Bear said to the poodle, who was watching him. He stood on his head, feet up, to show off his new shoes.

The poodle sniffed. 'You can't be in fashion without a hat! Didn't you know? All smart people have hats!'

So Bear wanted a hat next. But what excuse could he find this time?

'Maggie!' he said. 'I feel cold on my head . . .'

Maggie looked at him and went off to find a little sun-hat in the bottom of a drawer. She had worn it when she was a baby. It was just Bear's size.

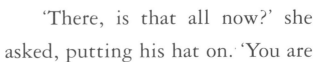

'There, is that all now?' she asked, putting his hat on. 'You are really becoming quite a Bothersome Bear!'

Bear sat with his hat on, thinking hard. What else was there that he must have and didn't have?

Just then the parrot woke up on his perch. He fixed a wicked eye on Bear. Suddenly he screeched, 'You do look silly! Just like a clown dressed up for the circus!'

Bear was very upset. Though he was all dressed up, he only made people laugh!

Then he had his second good idea – to throw off all those horrid clothes quickly! They were making him feel very uncomfortable and not at all like himself.

Up went his hat into the air. Off with those tight trousers! Shoes – away with them – one, two! He felt better and better every minute! The shirt and the ribbon went last. All the animals cheered.

Maggie's mother made a new cover for the old brown chair. Bear said, 'A brown bear shows up well on a flowery chair. I won't be sat on by mistake any more!'

But there was a bit of left-over flowery material. Maggie's mother made Bear a little dress out of it. So there he was again, a bear wearing the same pattern as the chair. And everyone was sure to sit on him as before.

BRAVE BEAR AND SCAREDY HARE

S. Mortimer

BEAR LIVED IN a cosy cave high in the mountains. Every morning he looked out to see if his friend Hare was awake.

'Morning, Hare,' said Bear to a pair of long brown ears sticking out of a burrow down the track. 'Where are you going today?'

'Down in the valley,' said Hare, blinking in the sunshine, 'to the edge of the woods where the wild carrots grow.'

'Oh,' said Bear, 'carrots again? I wonder you don't get tired of them.'

'No, no,' said Hare cheerfully, 'you can never have too many carrots.'

Bear smiled to himself. Hare said this every morning and he never saw her come home with a single carrot.

'I think I might come with you today,' said Bear.

'Oh no,' replied Hare in a hurry, 'there's nothing for a bear down there. You'd soon be bored.' She scampered off down the path, waving Bear a hasty goodbye.

Now Bear was curious, so he decided to follow his friend. He crept down the path after her, hiding behind trees. But Bear was a clumsy fellow and he soon walked straight into a low branch.

'SNAP!'

The branch broke off and flew down the mountain, whistling past Hare's ears.

'What was that?' said Hare, jumping behind a bush. She was so scared that her fur stood on end. She waited in the bush for some time before she was brave enough to come out.

By and by, Hare crept back on to the path. She started

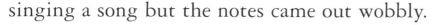

singing a song but the notes came out wobbly.

Behind his tree, Bear chuckled to himself. He couldn't believe what a scaredy hare his friend was. He looked forward to being able to tease her later.

Before long, Hare came to a stream. She looked at the water fearfully.

'Oh dear,' she sighed, 'it looks awfully dangerous and terribly cold.'

Just as Hare had plucked up the courage to swim across, she heard a large splash. She darted behind a nearby rock to hide.

Up on the path, Bear was rubbing his behind. He'd slipped on some pine needles and sent a rock flying into the water. His sides ached from giggling at his timid friend.

Bear waited and waited. At last, Hare shot out and dived into the stream, racing across to the other side.

'Juicy carrots, juicy carrots,' she said to herself at every stroke.

On the opposite bank, Hare shook herself dry and hurried down the path towards the edge of the woods. At last she saw a cluster of green carrot tops waving in the breeze and stood for a few moments, gazing at them longingly. She could almost taste their crunchy sweetness.

Hare had just started digging when she heard barking and scrambled up the nearest tree to hide. From the safety of the branches, she saw the same two mean-looking dogs that had always been near the carrot patch when she came each day. They trotted right up to the tree and flopped down to rest.

I'm done for, thought Hare miserably. She waited for what seemed like hours. By the time the dogs left, the last of the light was fading from the sky.

Bear thought the sight of Hare up a tree the funniest thing of all. He rolled around on the ground, hugging his sides, tears rolling down his face.

As he made his way back up the mountain, he was still chuckling at Hare. In fact, he was so preoccupied that he fell straight into a large hole in the ground. This wasn't funny at all.

'Help!' wailed Bear, as he looked up at the darkening sky above. 'HEEELLLPP!' His throat grew sore from shouting and

he began to feel scared.

After a while, he heard a little voice he knew. He looked up to see a large pair of brown ears sticking down the hole.

'Is that you, Bear?' said Hare, squinting into the darkness below.

'Hare, oh dear Hare. Can you help me?'

'Don't worry, Bear,' said Hare kindly. 'I have an idea.' She rolled a large log down the hill until it was on the edge of the hole.

'Stand back,' she shouted and gave the log a huge push.

Bear climbed out in no time and gave his friend a big hug. 'Thank you, Hare,' he said, 'you're the best friend a bear could ever have.'

'Oh, don't mention it, Bear,' said Hare blushing, 'I know you'd do the same for me.'

As the two friends made their way back home, Bear was very quiet. He felt a little ill in the pit of his stomach. It wasn't something he'd eaten and it wasn't because of his fall into the hole. It was his conscience troubling him. He thought of how much he'd laughed at Hare. He hadn't been a good friend to her at all.

The next morning, as Hare woke in her snug burrow, she could smell the most delicious smell. What could it be? She popped her head out to see a large pile of carrots lying on the grass.

'Morning, Hare,' said Bear from up in his cave.

'Morning, Bear. Are these from you?'

'Yes, I saw them when I was out blackberry picking and thought I might save you the journey to the field today.'

'How kind of you, Bear. You're the best friend a Hare could ever have.'

And Hare never had to go to the edge of the woods ever again. Each morning she woke up to the smell of carrots and found a large mouth-watering pile of them outside her burrow.

Bear still found plenty to laugh about but never at his friend Hare . . . well, maybe just a little bit.

PANDA'S JOURNEY

Ed Johnson

THERE WAS ONCE a panda, who wished more than anything else that she could fly.

'If I could fly,' she said, 'I'd visit the moon and travel around the world.'

'Flying isn't so special,' sighed Harriet the flamingo. 'Your wings get tired. I'd stick to climbing trees.'

Kiko the panda didn't agree. 'But you can go anywhere you want,' she said jumping up and down. 'You can see the whole world.'

Preen the parrot yawned. 'You're not missing all that much,

believe me,' he said cracking a nut in his beak. 'It gets awfully cold on a long flight.'

'But there must be some amazing things to see from up in the air,' said Kiko. Preen was too busy tidying his feathers to listen to Kiko so she went off to find her friend Oz.

'Don't you wish you could fly, Oz?' she asked.

'Not really,' replied the ostrich nibbling some grass. 'I can run anywhere I want to get to.'

'But think of all the new friends you could make,' said Kiko excitedly.

'I have all the friends I need here,' said Oz. 'Some of us are fliers, Kiko, and some of us are not. I'm a runner and you're a climber. That's just the way it is. Who ever heard of a flying panda?'

Before Kiko had a chance to reply, Oz had buried her head in the sand. Kiko sighed and wandered off to talk to another friend who could fly.

'Batty, Batty,' Kiko called up to the fruit bat.

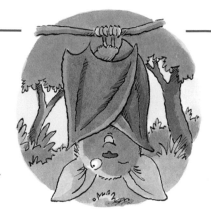

'What do you want? he answered sleepily. 'It's the middle of the night for me. Come back in a few hours' time. I'll be up when the sun goes down.'

That night, Kiko dreamed she had grown a beautiful pair of furry black and white wings. She was gliding over the forest, looking at her friends below who were pointing up at her.

Suddenly a bright flash of light woke her up. Rubbing her eyes, she padded off to explore.

The strange light came from deep within the forest. As she peered from behind a banana palm, Kiko saw a large rocket that had crashed into the trees. Two astronauts were busy mending something outside. Kiko couldn't believe her luck! She raced inside to explore and soon after, the door closed behind her and the great machine started to hum as the engine burst into life.

'Hooray!' she cried. 'I'll be able to see the world. I can fly after all.'

The rocket shot up into the air and Kiko was thrown against the wall and bumped her head. She began to feel dizzy

and rather sick. She looked outside the window but the rocket was moving so quickly, everything was a blur. Before long, her feet lifted off the ground and she began to float around in the air.

Oh dear! she thought as her tummy turned somersaults. This isn't so much fun after all.

'What's this?' cried one of the astronauts, coming out of the cockpit. 'A stowaway panda!'

Kiko looked green and rubbed her tummy.

'How did you get in here?' said the shocked astronaut. 'You don't look very well. Here, drink this.' He handed Kiko a silver plastic bag with a pink liquid inside. It didn't have much flavour but it seemed to settle her stomach. She thought sadly of her delicious bamboo trees back in the forest and the friends she had left behind. Maybe they were right and flying wasn't so great after all.

The rocket rushed up and up into the sky and very soon the earth below looked like a small marble. Kiko drifted off to sleep and when she woke, the rocket had landed. She looked out the window excitedly, expecting to see something familiar – some banana trees or her favourite clump of bamboo, but the world outside looked very different. There was nothing out there except hundreds of dusty craters and the two astronauts bouncing around in their space suits.

I'll never see my friends again, thought Kiko miserably. She waited for what seemed like days, but eventually the astronauts had finished their research and they headed back to earth.

'Hold on tight!' said the astronaut as the rocket shot into the air again. Kiko gripped on to a pole but she felt just as giddy on the way down as she had on the way up. The rocket landed in the sea with an enormous splash and Kiko said goodbye to the astronauts and swam to the shore.

When she had made her way back to the forest, she bumped into Batty, flying around looking for food. She was delighted to see her friend again.

'Hey, Kiko!' said Batty coming to sit in the panda's paw. 'Where have you been?'

'Hi, Batty,' she said smiling. 'Oh, you know, here and there.' Kiko knew that no one would believe where she'd really been.

'Didn't you want to ask me something?' said Batty.

'Did I?' replied Kiko pretending to be surprised. 'I can't think what it was. Probably nothing important.'

'Well, I'm off to find my breakfast. Bye.' And with one great flap of his black leathery wings he swooped away into the night.

Kiko couldn't wait to get her teeth into some tender bamboo and she headed off into the trees. She climbed in among the juicy green shoots and knew that this was the only place in the whole world she really wanted to be. She'd choose climbing over flying any day.

WHY BEAR HAS A STUMPY TAIL

A Norse tale, retold by Robert Scott

IN THE BEGINNING, and for a long time after the beginning, Bear had a magnificent tail. Bear had been at the back of the queue when ears were being handed out, so he got only small, stubby ears (though he could hear very well with them). He was so tired with queueing all day that he fell asleep as soon as he had been given his ears. When he woke up, he found that he was at the front of the queue for tails.

Bear chose the best tail there was. It was long and thick and wavy. He could use it to fan himself when he was hot and to keep off flies when they tried to torment him. He could wave

it, or lash it, or wag it. He even thought he might, possibly, be able to hold things with it if he tried hard enough.

Fox was very jealous. He was always up early and near the front of the queue when anything useful was being given out. He had been very near the front for ears, of course, and he had hoped to have the choice of tails. As it was, he got a very fine tail – but it was nowhere near as wonderful as Bear's.

One day, in the very depths of the very hardest of hard winters, when snow drifted deep in the fields and frost cracked among the treetops, Bear was searching for grubs under a rotten log and thinking it might be a good idea to sleep all winter and eat all summer when Fox suddenly appeared. He was carrying a string of stolen fish in his jaws.

'Where on earth did you get those?' Bear demanded. He loved fish but found it difficult to catch them.

Fox came to a sudden halt, then began to back slowly. He hadn't seen Bear behind the log and now there was a good chance that he would lose his fish.

'Well?' said Bear, moving closer.

'Shlishnig.'

'What?'

'Shlishnig.'

'Put them down and tell me properly,' Bear said.

Fox dropped the fish and placed a paw firmly and possess-
ively on top of them.

'Fishing,' he said. 'I caught them. Honest.'

'I wish I could catch fish like that,' said Bear, looking longingly at them. 'I don't suppose –'

'But of course I'll tell you how to do it,' Fox interrupted.
'With a tail like yours you'll catch loads and loads of fish.'

'Tail?' said Bear suspiciously. 'What's my tail got to do with it?'

'Well, I caught these in a couple of hours and my tail's not
nearly as big and bushy as yours. Of course, it smarted a bit
and got very cold, but there you are. The longer you stick it,

the more you catch. Well, I'll leave you to it then. See that –
Now, what's the matter?'

Bear was suddenly very close. He put his face even closer.

'You have not,' he said, 'even *begun* to explain yourself.'

'I haven't?' said Fox. 'Oh, I'm sorry. I thought I had. What
didn't you understand?'

'All of it,' said Bear. 'And especially the
bits you missed out.'

'Oh. Right. Well, first of all you go down
to the river. All right?'

'All right.'

'Or lake.'

'Or lake.'

'Or sea.'

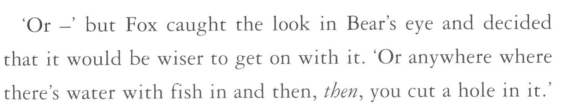

'Or sea.'

'Or –' but Fox caught the look in Bear's eye and decided
that it would be wiser to get on with it. 'Or anywhere where
there's water with fish in and then, *then*, you cut a hole in it.'

'In the water?'

'In the *ice*! It's winter, remember? You cut a hole in the ice
and lower your tail through and wave it about a bit to attract
attention. Then you just wait. For as long as you can. Of

course, as I said, it stings and smarts a bit, but that's just the fish biting. The longer you wait, the more fish you get. I caught all these in just two hours. Someone with your patience and with a tail like yours – why, I shouldn't be surprised if you couldn't stay out all night and break the record.'

'It sounds easy enough,' said Bear. 'What's the catch?'

'Enough fish to last you for weeks,' said Fox, 'but there is just one thing.'

'Oh?' said Bear suspiciously. 'What's that?'

'Well, there's no point in taking your tail out slowly. If you do, the fish will just drop off. When you've finished you have to give the strongest jerk you can. Pretend you're trying to jump over the moon. Then all the fish come straight out on to the ice and all you have to do is collect them up.'

'Right!' said Bear firmly. 'You just drop by tomorrow and see what I'll have to show you.' And with that he hurried off down the hill to the nearest river.

Fox watched him for a moment, then picked up his fish and trotted off home.

Bear did exactly as he had been told. For the rest of that day and much of the night he sat with his tail dangling through the ice. He sat for so long that it was completely frozen in.

Then he gathered his feet beneath him, set his eye firmly on the moon now sinking palely behind the trees, and gave the biggest, strongest leap he had ever made. And his tail snapped off.

Bear rushed home howling to wait for Fox to show up, but he never did.

That is why, today, all bears have short, stumpy tails (and why foxes keep away from them).

There's a Bear in the Bath

Nanette Newman

L IZA LOOKED OUT of the window and saw a bear sitting in the garden, so she went outside and said, 'What are you doing in my garden?'

'I'm here for a visit,' said the bear.

'Why?' asked Liza.

'Why not?' asked the bear.

'I don't know,' said Liza.

'Exactly,' said the bear, 'and by the way – when bears come to visit they usually get invited in.'

'Oh, come in,' said Liza.

The bear looked round the kitchen.

'Would you like something to eat?' asked Liza.

'Like what?' asked the bear.

'Porridge,' said Liza.

'What makes you think bears like porridge?'

'Well,' said Liza, 'when Goldilocks went to the three bears' house . . .'

'Oh, that,' said the bear. 'You didn't believe any of that, did you? You'll be saying next that all bears like honey.' He poured himself a cup of coffee.

'What's your name?' asked Liza.

'Jam,' said the bear.

'Nobody is called Jam,' said Liza.

'I am,' said the bear. 'My mother loved jam more than anything in the world,' said the bear, 'then she had me and she loved me more than anything in the world, so she called me Jam.'

'I see,' said Liza – not seeing at all – 'it just seems a funny name for a bear.'

But the bear wasn't listening – he'd turned on the radio and was dancing and spilling crisps everywhere. He danced into the hall, and into the living room, and then lay down on the sofa.

'You're a good dancer,' said Liza.

'I know,' said the bear.

He picked up the newspaper.

'I'm brilliant at crosswords,' he said.

'That's showing off,' said Liza.

'What is?' asked the bear.

'Boasting about how good you are at something,' said Liza.

'Oh, no,' said the bear, 'boasting is very unattractive in a child – boasting when you're a bear is quite acceptable.'

'Really,' said Liza.

'Yes, really,' said the bear. 'Now – what is the word for something you can't stand – ten letters?'

'I don't know,' said Liza.

'Unbearable,' said the bear.

'That's brilliant,' said Liza.

'Yes, I told you I was,' smiled the bear.

He leaped up and started to dance again.

'I dance the tango best of all,' he said.

'What's the tango?' asked Liza.

The bear took a rose from the vase, placed it between his teeth, grabbed Liza round the waist and marched up and down the room

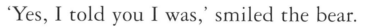

until she fell down in a breathless heap.

'Now that,' said the bear, 'was the tango. Of course, you have to practise a lot before you can do it as well as me. What's upstairs?' he said, already going up them.

'My room,' said Liza, as the bear flung open the door.

'It needs trees,' said the bear.

'Trees?' said Liza.

'Definitely,' said the bear. 'A few big trees growing in here would give it style, make it more like a forest.'

'But people don't have trees growing inside their rooms,' said Liza. 'And who'd want to live in a forest?'

'Bears,' said the bear, picking up Liza's school coat. He tried to put it on and it split right down the middle.

'Badly made,' said the bear, throwing it in the wastepaper basket.

'You were too big for it,' said Liza, wondering what she'd wear for school on Monday.

'No, no,' said the bear, 'if a coat doesn't fit a bear, there's something wrong with the coat – not something wrong with the bear. Always remember that.'

He went into the bathroom and climbed into the bath.

'This bath is too small,' said the bear.

'Well, it's big enough for me,' said Liza.

'What's the use of that if it's not big enough for a bear?' he said.

Liza heard her mother come in; she'd been chatting to the next-door neighbour.

'Time for tea,' she called upstairs.

'There's a bear in our bath,' shouted Liza.

'Is there, darling? That's nice. What's his name?'

'Jam,' shouted Liza.

'Oh, I forgot to get it. Never mind, I'll get some tomorrow.'

The bear was drinking hair shampoo and wearing a pair of frilly knickers on his head.

'How do I look?' he said.

'You look like a bear with a pair of frilly knickers on your head,' said Liza, but the bear had already disappeared into Liza's brother's room.

Jack was standing up in his cot, looking rosy from his nap.

'Teddy,' he said, pointing at Jam and dribbling with excitement.

'No, Jam,' said the bear. 'He's not very bright is he?'

'Well, he's only two,' said Liza.

'When I was two, I could count up to 1,104 and play the violin,' said the bear, scooping Jack out of his cot.

Liza's mother shouted up the stairs. 'Liza, have you finished your homework yet?'

'Mummy,' shouted Liza, 'there's a bear in Jack's room.'

'That's nice,' said her mother.

'I think it's time to go,' said the bear.

'Where to?' asked Liza.

'Oh, just somewhere,' said the bear, vaguely. 'I lead a very busy life, you know. I've got a singing lesson at four.'

'I didn't know that bears sang,' said Liza.

'Let's face it,' said the bear, 'you didn't know much about bears at all until you met me.'

'That's true,' said Liza.

'What will you do when I've gone?' asked the bear.

'I have to do my homework,' said Liza. 'I have to write about what I've done today.'

'That's easy,' said the bear. 'Just write that you met this totally wonderful, clever, fascinating bear.'

'No one would believe me,' said Liza.

And they didn't!

THE FUNNY STORY OF THE BEAR WHO WAS BARE

Nicola Baxter

ONCE THERE WAS a bear called Edwin Dalrymple Devereux Yeldon III. He said that his friends called him Eddy, but as a matter of fact, this bear did not have many friends at all. And that was because he was simply not a very nice bear. Oh, he was very handsome, with long, golden fur that shone in the sunlight, but that was where the problem began. Eddy thought he was better than other bears, with his long name and fancy fur.

'Pass me my fur brush,' he would say. 'The breeze has ruffled me terribly. You other bears need not worry, of course, with your short, rough, ordinary fur.'

When the bears played leap-bear or hide-and-seek in the nursery, Eddy always refused to play.

'Those are very rough games,' he complained. 'I might get my paws dirty. Games are too silly for superior bears like myself.'

Well, after a while, all the other bears were sick of Edwin and his airs and graces. I'm afraid that some young bears tried to think of ways of teaching Eddy a lesson. But as things turned out, they did not need to. Edwin Dalrymple Devereux Yeldon III brought about his own downfall.

One day, Eddy was boasting about all the famous bears he knew. One or two of the other bears wondered out loud if his tales were really true, which made Eddy furious. 'You'll see,' he said. 'I'll write a letter to my friend Prince Bearovski. He's sure to write back at once, and then you'll see.'

But as Eddy carried a huge bottle of ink across the room, his furry feet tripped on the edge of the rug. Down fell teddy Eddy. Up flew the bottle of ink. Splat! The bottle hit the floor and ink flew everywhere! There was ink on Eddy's nose and ink on his ears. His paws and his knees had bright blue splashes too.

For a second, there was silence. Then Eddy let out a horrible roar. 'You stupid bears!' he cried. 'Just look at my fur! Who put that rug in the way?' And that was really not very fair, for the rug had been there for years and years.

Teddy Eddy sulked for the rest of the day. But worse was to follow. Next morning, the little girl who lived there saw what

had happened to her most beautiful bear. Without asking anyone else at all, she decided that Eddy needed a bath.

The other bears peeked around the bathroom door to watch the proceedings. There were bubbles everywhere! Only the tip of teddy Eddy's nose could be seen. Giggling and chuckling, the bears went back to the nursery and waited for Eddy to reappear.

They waited all that day and all that night. But Eddy did not return. Next day, there was no sign of him.

'That little girl is not very sensible,' said one bear. 'She may have left him in the water. We really should go and see if he's all right, my friends.'

But teddy Eddy was not in the bathtub. The bears were just about to go away again, when one little bear noticed that one of the cupboards was not quite closed.

Inside sat Edwin Dalrymple Devereux Yeldon III, wrapped from ears to paws in a large towel.

'Come on, Eddy,' called the young bear mischievously, 'you must be dry by now.'

'No,' said Eddy. 'I . . . er . . . I can't.'

'But it must be very boring in this cupboard,' said another bear.

'No,' said Eddy. 'It's . . . er . . . very pleasant. Please go away.'

'Oh come on,' laughed two of the smallest bears. And they tugged playfully at the towel. Eddy tried hard to hold on to it, but it was no use. As the towel slipped away, every bear could see . . . Edwin Dalrymple Devereux Yeldon III was bare! When the little girl washed away the ink, Eddy's fur was washed away too.

Poor Eddy. He couldn't hide any more. Slowly, he walked back to the nursery and sat down in the darkest corner. The old, proud Edwin Dalrymple Devereux Yeldon III was gone. A very different bear remained.

For a few days, the other bears smiled to themselves about what had happened. But after a while, they began to feel rather sorry for Eddy.

'I think we should help him,' said one old bear. 'Apart from anything else, he must be cold without his fur.'

'That's true,' said another bear. 'Why don't we make him some clothes?'

Over the next few days, the bears had great fun. They used up all the old scraps of material that they could find and made some very grand clothes. There was a hat with a feather, a cloak with tassels, some striped trousers, and some shiny black boots.

When he saw them, Eddy was overwhelmed by the bears' kindness.

'Thank you, my friends,' he said, as he put on the clothes. 'I know that I have not been a very nice bear in the past, but I will try to do better now. In following all that is good and kind and bearlike, I will be absolutely fearless. Or per-haps I should say, in spite of my fine clothes, my dears, absolutely furless!'

Brer Bear's Grapevine

Lucy A. Cobbs & Mary A. Hicks

BRER BEAR USED to be very, very fond of grapes. He was a good farmer, so he went out into the woods and dug himself a grapevine and set it out on his farm.

Brer Bear tended his grapevine like it was a baby, hoeing and watering it in the summertime, and wrapping it up in the wintertime.

This went on for two years, and Brer Bear was really proud of himself when he saw the flowers on it the third spring that rolled around. He

went into the house that morning and he said to old Missus Bear, 'I am going to have the best grapes you ever saw this autumn, you just wait and see.'

Missus Bear started to grumble because she was ill-natured anyhow, and she said, 'You ought to make some grapes, you nurse that old vine all the time. I suppose that the birds will eat them up before they get ripe, though.' Brer Bear said, 'You are the crossest woman I've ever seen. You wouldn't see a bit of sunshine in a pot of gold, that's what you wouldn't and I know it.' With that he went back out to the grapevine.

Brer Possum came along and stopped to watch Brer Bear working. When he saw that Brer Bear really had himself a grapevine, he laughed to himself. Then he just went on about his business because the grapes weren't ripe yet.

The summer wore on, with Brer Bear always nursing that grapevine and watching the little grapes grow. When they began to grow and when they started turning purple, Brer Bear was so proud that all day long he watched them to see that the birds didn't peck at them. Meanwhile, Missus Bear just fussed and fussed at all the work he was putting in.

Brer Bear's grapes were ripening. One day, he said to himself that he wanted to eat some of them, but he just ate a few, because he wanted them to get nice and ripe before he ate them all up.

That same evening, Brer Possum woke up from a long nap and remembered the grapes and decided to go and see for himself how they were coming along. He sneaked up to the

garden where the vines were and he looked around for Brer Bear. When he saw that Brer Bear wasn't anywhere to be seen, he sneaked up and tasted one of the grapes. He just meant to taste the grapes to see if they were sweeter than the woods' grapes as Brer Bear said they were, but they were so good that Brer Possum kept on tasting them for a long time.

After a while, Brer Possum heard somebody coming and he climbed up on top of the vine just as Brer Fox crept up and started eating Brer Bear's grapes quietly. Brer Possum lay there quietly until Brer Fox got a taste and left, then he started eating again.

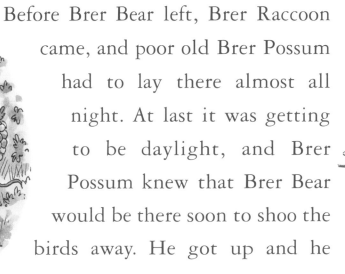

Soon he heard somebody else coming and he had to hide again. This time it was Brer Bear's cousin, and I tell you, this Brer Bear could sure say grace over a powerful heap of grapes.

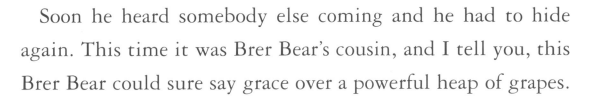

Before Brer Bear left, Brer Raccoon came, and poor old Brer Possum had to lay there almost all night. At last it was getting to be daylight, and Brer Possum knew that Brer Bear would be there soon to shoo the birds away. He got up and he

couldn't see any grapes to save his life, but when he heard Brer Bear opening the door he jumped off the vine, and I tell you he flew away from there.

Brer Bear, when he found he didn't have any grapes left, he went wild, at first with grief, then with anger, and he began to look for tracks of the thief. The other animals had stepped lightly but Brer Possum when he had jumped off the vine had planted his tracks in the soft dirt and there was no mistake about that being old Brer Possum himself that had left the tracks.

Brer Bear was so angry that he looked for Brer Possum for a

week to punish him but Brer Squirrel warned Brer Possum and Brer Possum stayed hidden for a long spell. He had another advantage too, for Brer Possum slept during the daytime and Brer Bear slept at night.

After that, Brer Bear never planted another grapevine and he never had any use for Brer Possum any more either. Until this day, they don't have a thing to do with each other, and Brer Possum is scared of Brer Bear. Of course, Missus Bear said to old Brer Bear, like a woman will, 'Old man, I told you so, didn't I?'

PINK FOR POLAR BEAR

Valerie Solís

NANOOK THE POLAR BEAR was not white like her brother and sister. Her fur was pink.

Some of the big polar bears said that Nanook was different because she had been born at sunset. They thought the sun's pink rays had coloured her fur. Her family called her Nanook, the 'daughter of the setting sun'.

'Who has ever heard of a pink polar bear?' said a very large and curious bear. The other bears laughed.

Nanook felt sad and lonely. She very much wanted to be a white polar bear like all the others.

'Maybe I am not a real polar bear at all?' she thought sadly. 'Polar bears love to chase seals, swim and catch fish. I don't like chasing the poor seals, and I'm not much good at swimming or catching fish.'

One day a terrific snowstorm blew up as Nanook and her family were coming home after a day's fishing.

The wind howled and raged all over the North Pole. The snow fell so thickly that Nanook couldn't see a thing as she struggled to keep up with her family.

'I'm so tired. The wind is far too strong. Perhaps I should rest and catch up with the others later,' she thought.

Nanook curled up in the snow and before long she fell into a deep sleep.

The next morning, Nanook awoke to find herself covered in snow.

'Oh dear! I must have slept for hours!' she thought.

Then she realized that she was all alone on an iceberg floating out to sea.

'Oh no! My family will never find me now!' she exclaimed.

Nanook floated further and further out to sea. Soon she began to feel very hungry.

She thought for hours about jumping into the sea to catch

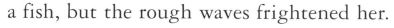

a fish, but the rough waves frightened her.

Suddenly Nanook heard a cry above her.

A beautiful plump fish dropped out of the sky at her feet.

Nanook looked up and saw Gullak, the seagull.

'Oh, thank you a million times, Gullak, thank you!' shouted Nanook.

'You're welcome,' replied Gullak.

Every day, Gullak caught the biggest and best fish for Nanook.

Gullak was a great storyteller as well as a great friend.

Nanook loved to listen to his tales about mermaids, flying fish, singing humpback whales, shipwrecks and many other fantastic things he had seen in his lifetime.

Nanook missed Gullak a lot when he wasn't around. There was nothing much to do on an iceberg except count other icebergs. Sometimes, Nanook saw some seals or walruses but they were either sleeping or too far away to hear her.

One night, beautiful melodies echoed all over the North Pole, waking Nanook from her dreams.

It was the singing humpback whales!

Suddenly, a great spray of water blew high into the air and a family of whales appeared near Nanook's iceberg.

'You must be the humpback whales that Gullak talks about!' cried Nanook. 'Your songs are beautiful! I wish I could sing like you and be heard far away. Then I would never be lonely.'

'And so you shall,' replied the largest whale called Fluke. 'We give you the "gift of song". From now on, you will be able to talk to us by singing, no matter how far away we are. You will never feel lonely again, Nanook, daughter of the setting sun.'

Then music filled Nanook's heart and she burst into song.

Her voice was as sweet as a nightingale.

The delighted whales blew great fountains of water into the air to show their pleasure, and set off on their long journey to other seas.

From that moment Nanook never stopped singing.

She sang to the humpback whales as they travelled to distant seas. The starry skies echoed with her sweet songs.

Nanook, the daughter of the setting sun, was talked about all over the North Pole and beyond.

Seals, seagulls and walruses travelled many miles just to hear her sing. Nanook was very happy.

One day Nanook had a great surprise. A large iceberg was

floating silently towards her.

'Ahoy, there!' a voice called out.

Nanook stopped singing.

'Hello!' she called back. But she could see nothing through the heavily falling snow.

'Ahoy, there!' the mysterious voice shouted again.

This time it came from right beside her.

'A blue polar bear!' exclaimed Nanook, peering through the snow.

'Hello, Nanook, daughter of the setting sun,' said the bear.

'Hello, but how do you know my name?' she asked.

'Ah! Nanook, the Singing Bear is famous throughout the North Pole,' answered the bear as he jumped on to Nanook's iceberg.

'Really? And who are you?' asked Nanook.

'My name is Koonan, son of the midday sky. I have been travelling on this iceberg for a long time listening to your enchanting music. Your voice is so beautiful that I closed my eyes and made a wish. And now I am here,' said Koonan.

'What was your wish?' asked Nanook.

'I wished with all my heart that you would sing especially for me,' replied Koonan.

'Of course,' she said, delighted. 'I shall sing the sweetest song of all just for you, Koonan.'

Koonan threw his arms into the air with joy and began to dance gracefully.

'Auuk, auuk!'

There was a cry above them.

Gullak dropped two plump fish to celebrate the beginning of a special friendship.

Nanook thought she was so lucky to have such marvellous friends.

Gullak had fed her and told her tales, and the whales had given her a wonderful gift of song. Now she had found Koonan, a very special bear friend.

'I'm glad I am me. I don't mind if I'm not a real polar bear after all,' she said.

'What do you mean?' asked Koonan. 'You look exactly like a polar bear to me. A very colourful polar bear.'

Nanook thought for a few moments.

The setting sun's rays turned her fur even pinker.

'Yes,' she said. 'And so are you!'

And together they laughed with happiness.

THE WREN AND THE BEAR

Grimm, translated by
Kevin Crossley-Holland

ONE SUMMER DAY the bear and the wolf were walking in
the forest when the bear heard the most beautiful bird-
song.

'Brother Wolf,' he said, 'what bird is that singing so
beautifully?'

'That's the king of the birds,' said the wolf. 'We all have to
bow down before him.' But it was only the wren.

'If that's the case,' said the bear, 'I'd like to have a look at
his royal palace; come and show me the way.'

'It's not as simple as that,' said the wolf. 'You'll have to wait until the queen gets back.'

Soon afterwards, the queen arrived with food in her beak, and so did the king, to feed their chicks. The bear would have liked to follow them there and then, but the wolf tugged at his sleeve and said, 'No, you must wait until the king and queen have gone away.'

So they kept an eye on the hole where the nest was, and then they went for a stroll. But the bear was restless: he wanted to see the palace and after a short while went back to the hole.

The king and queen had really left the nest now. The bear peered into the hole and saw five or six chicks lying in it.

'Is this the royal palace?' cried the bear. 'It's a miserable palace! And you're not princes or princesses, you're deceitful children.'

When the little wrens heard that, they flew into a terrible rage and cried, 'No, we're not, our parents are honest people. Bear, we're going to get even with you for this.'

The bear and the wolf were anxious; they made off and

gloomed in their lairs. But the little wrens went on shouting and screaming, and when their parents came back with food, they said, 'We won't touch a fly! Not even a tiny leg! Unless it's decided whether or not we're honest children, we'll starve to death. The bear has been here and insulted us.'

Then the old king said, 'Keep calm, everything will be put right.'

He flew off with his queen to the bear's lair and shouted in, 'Why have you insulted our children, you old growler? You're going to have to pay for this; we'll settle this in a fight to the finish.'

So war was declared on the bear and he summoned all the four-footed beasts: the ox, the donkey, the cow, the stag, the deer, and everything else that walks on earth.

But the wren summoned everything that flies in the air: not only the big and small birds, but also the gnats, hornets, bees and flies were called into action.

Now when the time of the battle drew near, the wren sent out scouts to find out who was Commander-in-Chief of the enemy. The gnats were the most cunning of all; they swarmed into the forest where the enemy was drawing up, and one finally settled under a leaf of the very tree where the orders were being handed down.

The bear was standing there. He called the fox to them and said, 'Fox, you're the most cunning of all the animals. You must be General and lead us.'

'All right,' said the fox. 'So what shall we take as the signal to begin?'

Nobody was able to think of anything.

'I have a beautiful long bushy tail,' said the fox, 'and it looks much the same as a plume of red feathers. When I hold up my tail, our chances will be good and you must advance; but if I let it drop, then take to your heels.'

When the gnat heard that, she flew back and disclosed every scrap of information to the wren.

When the day of the battle dawned – Oh! Then the four-footed beasts came pounding along to the battlefield so that the earth trembled; and the wren and his army converged on that place through the air so that it purred and cried and whirred, and struck fear and terror into the heart. And so both sides attacked one another.

Then the wren despatched the hornets with orders to sit under the fox's tail and sting him for all they were worth. Now when the fox was stung for the first time, he winced and raised one leg, but he bore the pain and went on holding his tail erect; at the second sting, he had to drop it for a moment; but at the third sting, he could no longer bear the pain, cried out and let his tail fall between his legs. When the animals saw that, they thought that all was lost and took to their heels, each to his own lair; and so the birds had won the battle.

Then the king and queen flew home to their children and called out, 'Be happy, children. Eat and drink to your hearts' content; we have won the war.'

'No, we won't eat yet,' said the little wrens. 'First the bear must come to our nest and ask for our forgiveness and say that we are honest children.'

So the wren flew to the bear's den and called out, 'You must come to the nest, growler, and beg my children's forgiveness and tell them that they are honest children, or we'll break every rib in your body.'

Hearing this, the bear dragged himself along in utter terror and begged for forgiveness. Only now were the little wrens satisfied. They sat themselves down and ate and drank and made merry until late that night.

FATHER BEAR AND THE NAUGHTY BEAR CUBS

Margaret Mayo

ONCE UPON A TIME there was a Father Bear who lived in a cave with his two little bear cubs.

Every day Father Bear had to go into the forest to hunt for food, and every day, while he was away, the little bears were naughty. They splashed in puddles until they looked like wet washing. They wandered off and got lost. They growled and quarrelled.

One day, when their father had gone hunting, the two little bears went for a walk in the forest. By and by, they came to a muddy patch, and — guess what they did. They jumped

SPLOSH! Straight into the mud and stomped about SQUISHY-SQUASHY! SQUELCH! SQUELCH! until they looked like two sticky mud cakes.

After a while, Grandmother Fox came trotting along. 'You naughty bears!' she said. 'What will your father say when he sees you?'

But the little bears laughed and sang out, 'We don't care! Old Granny Bushy-tail, we don't care!'

Grandmother Fox was very cross. 'I shall tell your father about you,' she said. And she did just that.

'Oh dear! Oh dear!' sighed Father Bear. 'I must find someone to take care of my little bears while I am away. They are much too young and foolish to be left on their own.'

So, next morning, Father Bear filled a sack with honey cakes, slung it over his shoulder, and walked off into the forest. He had not gone far when he met a black crow.

'Where are you going with a sack on your back?' said the black crow.

'I am looking for someone to take care of my little bears while I am away from home,' said Father Bear.

'And what's in the sack?' asked the black crow.

'Honey cakes,' said Father Bear. 'Three honey cakes a day are the wages.'

'For three honey cakes a day, I'd take care of them,' said the black crow.

'Ah! But would you know how?' said Father Bear. 'They can be very naughty.'

'Of course I know how,' said the black crow.

'I'd open my sharp beak and screech, CAW! CAW! CAW! That would soon make them behave.'

'Black crow,' said Father Bear, 'you are not the sort of person I am looking for. You would frighten my little bears.'

Father Bear walked on, and before long he met a grey wolf.

'Where are you going with a sack on your back?' said the grey wolf.

'I am looking for someone to take care of my little bears

while I am away from home,' said Father Bear.

'And what's in the sack?' asked the grey wolf.

'Honey cakes,' said Father Bear. 'Three honey cakes a day are the wages.'

'For three honey cakes a day, I'd take care of them,' said the grey wolf.

'Ah! But would you know how?' said Father Bear. 'They can be very naughty.'

'Of course I know how,' said the grey wolf. 'I'd show them my sharp teeth and howl *owww! owww! owww!* That would soon make them behave.'

'Grey wolf,' said Father Bear, 'you are not the sort of person I am looking for. You would frighten my little bears.'

Father Bear walked on, and before long he met a brown hare.

'Where are you going with a sack on your back?' said the brown hare.

'I am looking for someone to take care of my little bears while I am away from home,' said Father Bear.

'And what's in the sack?' asked the brown hare.

'Honey cakes,' said Father Bear. 'Three honey cakes a day are the wages.'

'For three honey cakes a day, I'd take care of them,' said the brown hare.

'Ah! But would you know how?' said Father Bear. 'They can be very naughty.'

'Of course I know how to take care of little bears,' said the brown hare. 'I would say HUSH! HUSH! HUSH! Then I would play with them and tell them stories. And if they were cross, I would tickle their tummies, and when they were tired, I would cuddle them close.'

'Brown hare,' said Father Bear, 'you are just the sort of person I am looking for. You will love my little bears, and they will love you.'

'But first I must look at those honey cakes!' said the brown hare. Father Bear put the sack on the ground and opened it, and the brown hare poked in her head and she sniff-sniff-sniffed!

'Those are good honey cakes!' she said. 'And three a day will suit me fine.'

'Then that's agreed!' said Father Bear.

He slung the sack over his shoulder and made for home, and the brown hare leaped along beside him.

When they reached the cave, Father Bear said to his cubs, 'Here is the brown hare. She will take care of you when I am away from home. So listen to her and try to be good.'

'Oh! We will try!' said the little bears. 'We will!'

After that, whenever Father Bear went off to hunt for food in the forest, the brown hare took care of the little bears. She played with them and told them stories. She tickled their tummies and cuddled them close. Every single day.

And the little bears listened to what she said, and they tried to be good. At least . . . most of the time, they did!

THE BEAR MAN

James Riordan

THERE WAS ONCE a boy of the Pawnee nation, settled in what is now called Oklahoma, who would imitate the ways of the bear. When he played with the other boys of his village he pretended to be a bear; he even told them he could turn himself into a bear whenever he liked. He came to act this way because of his father; and this is his story.

Before the boy was born, his father had gone hunting not far from the camp and had come upon a wounded bear cub. The tiny furry creature was so helpless that the man could not pass by and let it die. So he stooped down and tied some Indian tobacco round its neck saying:

'The Great Spirit, Tirawa, will take care of you. This tobacco charm will help you. I hope, in turn, that your fellow bears will one day take care of my son when he is born, and help him grow into a great and wise man.'

With that, he left the bear cub and returned to the camp.

He told his wife of the encounter with the bear cub: how he had looked into its eyes and talked to it. Now, there is a Pawnee superstition that, before a child is born, the child's parents must not look at an animal or think too much about it, or else the child will inherit its ways. And when the boy was born, his habits resembled those of a bear; he became more and more like a bear as he grew older.

He would frequently wander into the forest by himself and pray to the Great Bear Spirit.

When he had grown to man-hood, he led a Pawnee war party against their enemies the Sioux. Unsuspecting, however, they walked straight into an ambush and were killed, every last man of them.

Now, that part of the country was rocky and full of cedar trees, with many bear dens round about. It was not long before some bears came upon the dead bodies and discovered that of the Bear Man. A she-bear recognized it at once as that of the man who had prayed to the Bear Spirit, sacrificed tobacco to them, made up songs about them, and had done them many a good turn.

She collected the remains of the Bear Man, whose body had been strewn across the plain; placing all the parts together, she lay down upon his body and worked her medicine on him

until he showed signs of life. At length, he recovered enough to be led, still very weak, to the she-bear's den.

During his time with the bears he was taught all the things they knew – which was a great deal, for the people know that the bear is the wisest of animals. The bears told him that all he had learned was the gift of Tirawa, who had made the bears and given them their strength and wisdom. He was instructed never to forget the bears, nor cease to imitate them, for that would determine his success as a wise and powerful leader.

Finally, the she-bear told him this:

'The cedar tree shall be your protector. It never grows old, is ever fresh and green, it is Tirawa's gift. If a thunderstorm comes while you are at home with your family, throw some cedar wood upon the fire and you will all be safe.'

When he arrived home, the young man was greeted with joy and astonishment, for everyone thought he had died with the rest of the war party. He at once told the tribe of how the bears had saved him and next day he took

gifts of tobacco, beads, buffalo meat and sweet-smelling clay to present to them. The she-bear hugged him and spoke these words:

'As my fur has touched you, you will be great. As my hands have touched you, you will be fearless. As my mouth touches your mouth, you will be wise.'

With that they parted for the last time.

In the passing of time, the Bear Man did indeed become the greatest warrior of his tribe. He was the originator of the Bear Dance, which the Pawnees still practise to this day.

TEDDY BEAR GETS TOO FAT FOR HIS JACKET

Margaret Gore

ONE MORNING WHEN Teddy Bear was doing up his dark blue jacket with the three brass buttons, the middle button popped off and fell on the floor.

'Oh dear,' said Teddy Bear in his deep, growly voice. 'I must be getting fat.'

He looked at himself in the mirror.

'Either I have got fat or the jacket has shrunk. Perhaps it shrank when I got caught in all that rain the other day.'

Then Teddy Bear remembered that he had been wearing his green pullover that day.

'There is no doubt about it,' said Teddy Bear. 'I have got too fat and I shall have to do some exercises.'

But by the time Teddy Bear had done arm stretch three times and knees bend twice, he was quite out of breath.

'Oh dear,' he growled. '*That* won't do. I shall have to think of something else. Perhaps my friend Badger can help me.'

So down to the common went Teddy Bear – left, right, left, right, left, right. He found Badger busily digging in the earth.

'Please, Badger, can you help me?' asked Teddy Bear. 'I've got too fat and I can't do up my jacket.'

'You should try digging holes as I do, Teddy Bear,' said Badger.

So Teddy Bear took off his jacket and began digging. He was tired out after digging up only about one pailful of earth.

'Oh dear,' growled Teddy Bear. '*That* won't do. I don't think bears are meant to dig holes. I'll have to think of something else. Perhaps my friend Brown Dog can help me.'

So off went Teddy Bear again – left, right, left, right, left, right – till he came to the crossroads.

'Please can you help me, Brown Dog?' asked Teddy Bear.

'I've got too fat and I can't do up my jacket.'

'You should do as I do, Teddy Bear,' replied Brown Dog. 'I am always running about – I hardly ever stop except when I go to bed.'

So Teddy Bear ran all the way home, but when he arrived he was so breathless he had to sit down in his armchair and have a few spoonfuls from a tin of sweet milk to make him feel better.

'Oh dear,' growled Teddy Bear. '*That* won't do. I don't think bears are meant to keep on running all the time without stopping. I'll have to think of something else. Perhaps my friend Tabcat will be able to help me.'

Down the road he went again – left, right, left, right, left, right – till he came to Tabcat's home.

He saw Tabcat sitting on top of the high wall that went round his garden.

'Can you help me, Tabcat?' asked Teddy Bear. 'I've got too fat and I can't do up my jacket.'

'You should try jumping, Teddy Bear,' replied Tabcat, looking down at him with his green eyes. 'I am always jumping up on to this wall.'

'Jumping?' said Teddy Bear doubtfully.

Tabcat looked at Teddy Bear's fat little figure standing there and he said kindly: 'Perhaps you could start jumping on to little walls first, Teddy Bear. Come with me.'

Tabcat jumped gracefully down from the high wall and led Teddy Bear into the rose garden.

'There you are, Teddy Bear, there's a nice low wall,' said Tabcat. 'Now if you'll excuse me, it's time for my lunch.'

It may have been a low wall to Tabcat, but to Teddy Bear it looked quite high.

However, he went back a few steps, then took a flying leap at the wall. Unfortunately he didn't jump quite high enough and landed on the ground with a hard thud.

'Oooo! Oh dear,' growled Teddy Bear. 'I *certainly* don't think bears were meant to go jumping up on to walls – even if they are low ones.'

He walked sadly home, feeling rather stiff and sore.

On the way back he came to Mrs Duck's shop. Once a week he bought a large jar of honey at Mrs Duck's and today was the day for it.

'It's no use,' he said to himself. 'The only way I shall stop being fat is to give up eating sweet things. I must go in and tell Mrs Duck that I shall not be needing any more jars of honey. Oh dear!'

He gave a big sigh, for if there was one thing Teddy Bear did love it was honey.

'My goodness, Teddy Bear, you do look tired!' exclaimed Mrs Duck and she made him sit down on a chair.

'I do feel rather weak, Mrs Duck,' replied Teddy Bear. He cast a longing glance at a jar of honey on the shelf.

'Poor Teddy Bear, you probably need something to eat. I'll get you a big cup of cocoa and a chocolate biscuit. Then you'll feel better.'

Teddy Bear held up a weak paw. 'No, no thank you, Mrs Duck, I won't have anything,' he said.

Mrs Duck stared at Teddy Bear in astonishment. 'You must be ill, Teddy Bear,' she said. 'Perhaps I should call the doctor.'

Then Teddy Bear told her all his troubles and showed her

his jacket. 'It only means you are growing up into a fine big bear,' laughed Mrs Duck, 'and who ever heard of a *thin* bear! Now you just stay there and I shall sew on your buttons in a different place. I hope you haven't lost that middle button, Teddy Bear?'

'Oh no, Mrs Duck,' replied Teddy Bear. 'Here it is in my pocket.'

Mrs Duck sewed the buttons on one inch nearer the edge. 'Now, Teddy Bear,' she said, 'come and try your jacket.'

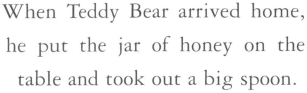

It was a perfect fit.

'Oh, thank you, Mrs Duck,' cried Teddy Bear. 'Now I must go home – and I'll take a jar of honey with me – a large jar.'

When Teddy Bear arrived home, he put the jar of honey on the table and took out a big spoon.

Then he gave a deep growly laugh.

'Who ever heard of a *thin* bear!' he said.

WHITE BEAR'S SECRET

Martine Beck

EVER SINCE THEIR wedding, Brown Bear and White Bear had lived happily in their chalet high up on the mountainside.

One day, as they came back up from the village with some warm crusty bread and a basket full of fresh vegetables, it began to rain. 'Look, the snow's melting,' said White Bear. 'Winter's almost over.'

'The woods smell so wonderful when it rains,' added Brown Bear as they came indoors. They quickly took off their soaking-wet boots and damp clothes so they wouldn't catch cold.

They soon got a fire going to warm themselves up. Then Brown Bear put on his chef's apron and hat and made his speciality, which was spaghetti with oodles of tomato sauce.

After supper, they got down to a game of chess on a board that Brown Bear had made himself.

But as soon as he realized he was losing, Brown Bear yawned and stretched and said he couldn't keep his eyes open. They were snug as bugs as they nestled in their warm, comfortable bed. They read their favourite bear stories for a while and were soon fast asleep.

Suddenly, very early in the morning, they were woken up by a terrifying rumbling noise. Everything round them began to shake . . . and then the roof of the chalet collapsed on top of them.

Both Brown Bear and White Bear were knocked unconscious. When Brown Bear came round, he found himself pinned under some beams. He worked himself free and clambered over to his wife. White Bear was lying very still. Their

friend the owl, who was perched on the branch of a larch, saw the terrible avalanche as it swept down the mountainside. She immediately flew off to the village to raise the alarm.

'Come quickly!' she cried. 'The avalanche has destroyed Brown Bear's chalet!' The villagers immediately grabbed pickaxes, forks and shovels, and scrambled as fast as they could up the mountain path to the chalet.

The chalet was a jumble of beams and debris and broken glass. White Bear was lifted out, and soon came round. Fortunately she had only fainted. She was given a small glass of elderberry cordial to make her feel better. Brown Bear meanwhile was having his cuts and bruises attended to, though a glass of cordial would have been far more to his liking!

A few of the villagers then went to fetch blankets, and some steaming hot soup to warm everyone up. Before dark, a tent was put up so that Brown Bear and White Bear could sleep out without feeling too cold. 'How can we ever thank you enough?' Brown Bear called out to his friends, as they went back down the mountainside.

In the morning, the village bears piled a cart high with all the planks, nails, hammers and saws needed to rebuild the chalet. Then they pushed it up the steep path. Brown Bear and White Bear were in the middle of breakfast when they saw their friends appear. Everyone soon got down to work.

Tap, rap, thump, knock, bang . . .

There were bears sawing, sand-papering, planing, hammering and nailing. Slowly but surely the chalet took shape again.

White Bear, however, was feeling very tired these days: she felt giddy and a bit sick.

'Why am I feeling like this?' she wondered.

'Are you all right?' asked a worried Brown Bear.

'It's a secret, but I think . . .'

'Are you sure? A baby bear?' Brown Bear was quite over-come. 'I am so happy,' he said.

White Bear dozed for hours in the spring sunshine, dreaming of the baby bear she could feel kicking inside her. But she also kept her eye on all the work being done in the house.

One fine spring day, the chalet was finished at last. 'It's even more beautiful than before,' said White Bear. Brown Bear went up on the roof to plant a young fir tree in the chimney and everyone celebrated with a marvellous picnic.

Now it was time to prepare for the baby. Brown Bear made a pretty rocking cradle and White Bear embroidered some pillowcases with green fir trees. That evening, after a delicious dinner by candlelight, they watched a fascinating programme on the life of polar bears.

A few weeks later, White Bear was singing an aria from an opera, accompanied by Brown Bear on the piano, when the baby started kicking in time to the music. 'I think he wants to come into the world,' said White Bear. Brown Bear phoned the midwife: 'Come 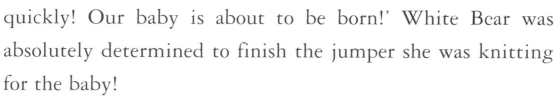 quickly! Our baby is about to be born!' White Bear was absolutely determined to finish the jumper she was knitting for the baby!

A few hours later, Brown Bear and White Bear's son was born. 'He is the most beautiful little bear cub in the world,' Brown Bear said to White Bear. 'How lucky we are!'

SNOW-WHITE AND ROSE-RED

Traditional

APOOR WIDOW ONCE lived in a lonely cottage with two rose trees in the garden, one of which had white flowers and the other red. She had two daughters, one called Snow-White and the other Rose-Red. Often the sisters went into the woods to gather berries, and the wild animals did them no harm.

Snow-White and Rose-Red kept their mother's cottage so tidy that it was a pleasure to see it. In summer Rose-Red looked after the house and every morning put by her mother's bed a spray of roses from both rose trees. In the winter Snow-White lit the fire and put on the kettle and, in the evening, the sisters sat by the fire and their mother put on her spectacles and read aloud out of a big book.

One evening, as they sat together, someone knocked at the door. 'Quick, Rose-Red,' said her mother, 'see who is there.'

Rose-Red unbolted the door, thinking it was a poor man outside, but it was a bear who pushed his great black head inside! Rose-Red screamed and jumped back, but the bear said, 'Don't be afraid; I shan't hurt you. I am frozen and only want to warm myself.'

'Poor bear,' said the mother. 'Lie down close to the fire.' Then she called, 'Snow-White, Rose-Red, come here. The bear will do you no harm.'

So they came close, and the bear said, 'Children, please knock the snow off my coat.'

They fetched a broom and brushed the snow off, and the bear stretched himself out by the fire.

Before long they were all the best of friends, the children pulled his hair, put their feet on his back, pushed him about and laughed when he growled. The bear enjoyed it too.

When bedtime came, the bear slept by the fire and, in the

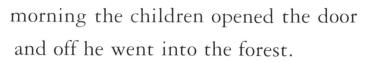

morning the children opened the door and off he went into the forest.

After that the bear came every evening at the same time, lay down by the fire, and let the children tease him as much as they liked.

When spring came, the bear said one morning, 'I must go away now, and I shan't be back all summer.'

Snow-White was very sad to say goodbye to the bear. He hurried away and was soon hidden among the trees.

Not long afterwards the two children were sent by their mother into the wood to gather sticks. Close by a fallen tree, they saw something jumping about in the grass. When they came nearer they saw it was a dwarf with a long white beard. The end of his beard was caught in a split in the wood, and the dwarf was leaping to and fro but couldn't get away.

He glared at the girls and shouted, 'What are you standing there for? Can't you come over here and help me?'

'What has happened to you, little man?' asked Rose-Red.

'Stupid, inquisitive goose!' answered the dwarf. 'I wanted to split the tree for firewood but my beautiful white beard got caught, and I can't get it out. And you silly milk-faced idiots just laugh!'

The children tried their best to help, but the beard was too tightly caught.

'Don't be impatient,' said Snow-White, and she took her scissors from her pocket and cut off the end of the beard.

The moment the dwarf was free he grabbed a bag full of gold that was lying at the roots of the tree and grumbled, 'Nice manners! Cutting off a piece of my fine beard! Bad luck to you.' And off he went without another word.

One day soon afterwards, Snow-White and Rose-Red went out to catch some fish. As they walked towards the river, they saw something that looked like a big grasshopper, jumping about by the water. They ran up and found it was the dwarf again.

'Surely you don't want to get into the river?' asked Rose-Red.

'Do you think I'm a fool?' answered the dwarf. 'Can't you see this brute of a fish is trying to pull me in.'

The dwarf had been fishing but the wind had tangled his beard in the fishing line. Then, when a big fish took the bait, the dwarf was not strong enough to pull it out and he was in great danger of being pulled into the water.

The girls had come just in time; they tried to free him, but couldn't. There was nothing to do but to bring out the scissors

and cut his beard again.

When the dwarf saw what had happened, he screamed, 'Is that a nice thing, you spiteful creature, to spoil my looks? As if it wasn't enough to clip my beard, now you've taken off the best part of it!' Then he brought out a sack of pearls from among the rushes and without another word, disappeared with it.

Another time, as they crossed a moor, the girls saw a big bird land not far away and then heard a sharp cry of terror. Running up, they saw with horror that an eagle was trying to carry off the dwarf. They pulled hard and hit the eagle until at last it let go and flew off.

Then the dwarf screamed, 'Couldn't you have been less rough? Look at my coat – it's all torn, you clumsy good-for-nothings.'

And he took up a sack of jewels and ran into his hole.

In the evening when the girls were on their way home they surprised the dwarf again. He had spread out all his treasures on an open space, not thinking that anyone would be passing there so late. The jewels sparkled so beautifully that the children stopped to admire them.

'What are you gaping at?' screamed the dwarf and his ashy-grey face turned red with rage. Suddenly a black bear trotted out of the forest. In terror the dwarf cried, 'Forgive me, good Mr Bear, and I'll give you all my treasures. Spare my life – I'm such a tiny little fellow, you'd never even taste me. Eat those two plump girls instead.'

The bear took no notice of his words but gave the spiteful creature a blow with his paw, and that was the end of him.

The girls were running away but the bear called after them, 'Snow-White and Rose-Red, don't be afraid! Wait for me.'

They recognized his voice, and then suddenly his bear's skin fell off and there stood a handsome man, all clothed in gold.

'I am a king's son,' he said. 'That horrible dwarf stole my treasures and changed me into a bear for as long as he lived.'

Snow-White married him and Rose-Red married his brother and they shared the treasure that the dwarf had collected. The old mother lived in comfort and happiness with her children. Of course, she took the two rose trees with her and planted them near her window and every year they bore lovely roses, white and red.

ACKNOWLEDGEMENTS

The publisher gratefully acknowledges the following, for permission to reproduce copyright material in this anthology:

'Baldilocks and the Six Bears' (shortened from the original for this edition) by Dick King-Smith from *The Ghost at Codlin Castle and Other Stories* published by Viking 1992, copyright © Fox Busters Ltd, reprinted by permission of A. P. Watt Ltd on behalf of Fox Busters Ltd; 'Ursula by the Sea' (shortened from the original for this edition) by Sheila Lavelle from *Ursula by the Sea* first published by Hamish Hamilton Children's Books 1986, copyright © Sheila Lavelle, 1986, reprinted by permission of Penguin Books Ltd; 'Elephant's Lunch' (shortened from the original for this edition) by Kate Walker from *The Teddy Bear Book* first published by Oxford University Press, Australia 1986, copyright © Kate Walker, 1986, reprinted by kind permission of the author; 'Not-So-Blue Bear' by Hiawyn Oram from *Not So Grizzly Bear Stories* first published by Orchard Books 1997, copyright © Hiawyn Oram, 1997, reprinted by permission of Orchard Books, a division of The Watts Publishing Group Ltd, 96 Leonard Street, London EC2A 4XD; 'Brown Bear in a Brown Chair' by Irina Hale, copyright © 1985, Irina Hale, reprinted by kind permission of Irina Hale c/o Laura Cecil Literary Agency; 'Brave Bear and Scaredy Hare' by S. Mortimer first published by Puffin Books 2000, copyright © S. Mortimer, 2000, reprinted by kind permission of the author; 'Panda's Journey' by Ed Johnson first published by Puffin Books 2000, copyright © Ed Johnson, 2000, reprinted by kind permission of the author; 'Why Bear has a Stumpy Tail' by Robert Scott from *The Oxford Book of Animal Stories* first published by Oxford University Press 1994, copyright © Robert Scott, 1994, reprinted by permission of Oxford University Press; 'There's a Bear in the Bath' (shortened from the original for this edition) by Nanette Newman from *There's a Bear in the Bath* first published by Pavilion Books Ltd 1993, copyright © Bryan Forbes Ltd, 1993, reprinted by kind permission of the author c/o Curtis Brown; 'The Funny Story of the Bear who was Bare' by Nicola Baxter from *The Teddy Bear Collection* first published by Armadillo Books 1998, copyright © Bookmart Ltd, 1998, reprinted by permission of Bookmart Ltd; 'Brer Bear's Grapevine' by Lucy A. Cobbs and Mary A. Hicks from *Animal Tales from the Old North State* first published by E. P. Dutton Inc. 1938, copyright © Lucy A. Cobbs and Mary A. Hicks, 1938, renewed 1966 reprinted by permission of Penguin Putnam Inc.; 'Pink for Polar Bear' by Valerie Solís from *Pink for Polar Bear* first published by Hamish Hamilton Children's Books 1996, copyright © Valerie Solís, 1996, reprinted by permission of Penguin Books Ltd; 'The Wren and the Bear' (originally entitled *The Hedge-king and the Bear*) by the Brothers Grimm, translated by Kevin Crossley-Holland and Susanne Lugert from *The Fox and the Cat Kevin Crossley-Holland's Animal Tales from Grimm* first published by Andersen Press Ltd 1985, copyright © Kevin Crossley-Holland and Susanne Lugert 1985, reprinted by permission of Rogers, Coleridge and White Ltd; 'Father Bear and the Naughty Bear Cubs' by Margaret Mayo from *How to Count Crocodiles* first published by Orion Children's Books 1994, copyright © Margaret Mayo 1994, reprinted by permission of Orion Children's Books; 'The Bear Man' by James Riordan from *The Songs my Paddle Sings* first published by Pavilion Books Ltd 1996, copyright © James Riordan 1995, reprinted by kind permission of Pavilion Books Ltd; 'White Bear's Secret' by Martine Beck from *White Bear's Secret* first published by L'école des Loisirs 1990, copyright © Martine Beck, 1990, reprinted by permission of David Grossman Literary Agency Ltd.

Every effort has been made to trace copyright holders but in a few cases this has proved impossible. The publisher apologizes for these cases of copyright transgression and would like to hear from any copyright holder not acknowledged.